GLASSES

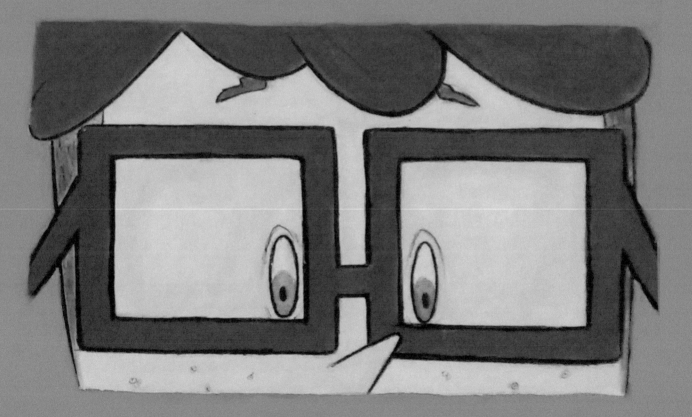

ROSA FRANCE

Illustrated by:
Caitlyn Livermore

AuthorHouse™
1663 Liberty Drive
Bloomington, IN 47403
www.authorhouse.com
Phone: 833-262-8899

Because of the dynamic nature of the Internet, any web addresses or links contained in this book may have changed since publication and may no longer be valid. The views expressed in this work are solely those of the author and do not necessarily reflect the views of the publisher, and the publisher hereby disclaims any responsibility for them.

Any people depicted in stock imagery provided by Getty Images are models, and such images are being used for illustrative purposes only.
Certain stock imagery © Getty Images.

This book is printed on acid-free paper.

ISBN: 978-1-6655-2456-8 (sc)
ISBN: 978-1-6655-2457-5 (e)

Print information available on the last page.

Published by AuthorHouse 05/20/2021

authorHOUSE®

GLASSES

Hello! My name is Griffin.

I am 10 years old.

I am 4 foot 10 inches, with fire red
hair and garden green eyes.

And the only way people know
me is my GLASSES.

Yep, I wear stupid GLASSES.

Dark brown, squared GLASSES.

In school people either called
me glasses or Dexter.

Why Dexter you ask?

Because they insisted I looked JUST LIKE
Dexter from Dexter's Laboratory.

Don't know what Dexter's Laboratory is?

Please look it up, then you'll
know why I don't like it!

One day I came home upset, and
my mom asked me why.

"People only look at me to make
fun of me and my glasses."

Mom said, "Your glasses are
what make you special!"

"Mom, you just don't understand."

"Griffin, help me understand."

"Mom, they just see me as a dork because of the way my glasses make me look."

"Well, what do you want to do about it hunny?"

"Can I get contacts?"

"No, but we can look at new glasses if you want?"

"Sure. All it could do is help."

The next week my mom took me to the eye doctor. The lady let me try on any that I wanted.

One pair caught my eye.

They were sky blue Ray-Ban glasses.

I looked at my mom and said "Mom what about these ones?

She looked at me and said, "Those ones, those are the ones you want."

"Yes, please!"

"Ok, you got it hunny."

A week later, I finally got my NEW glasses.

I was soooo excited to show them off at school.

The next day, I walked into school as slow as a snail I was so nervous.

When I walked into the doors, the unexpected happened...

Everyone was very friendly. As I walked through the hallway, people kept walking up to me and complimented me on my glasses.

"Griffin nice glasses!" "Griff lookin' good!" "Sweet shades!"

As the day went on, the compliments made me feel better about the way I look. As soon as I got home, Mom came to me and asked how school was."

I told her all about my day and the compliments people were giving me!

"Mom, I guess it's not so bad being Glasses after all!"

About the Author

Rosa France, the author of Glasses, grew up in a small town in New York, where she still resides. Rosa works as a Kindergarten teacher. She graduated from The State University of New York at Fredonia in the Spring of 2020, with a B.S.Ed. in Early Childhood/ Childhood Education, concentrating in English. In her spare time, Rosa enjoys reading, writing and spending time with her family. She started writing children's books at a young age, but didn't believe her work was good enough to publish, until she met one of her professors in college, who encouraged her to "reach for the stars!"

About the Illustrator

Western New York is home to Caitlyn Livermore where she paints photo realism and teaches private art classes to people of all ages. She has a fine art/studio art degree which helped give her the skills to become a full-time artist/designer and illustrator. Caitlyn is mostly commissioned to paint portraits, pets, cartoons, and landscapes.

Printed in the United States
by Baker & Taylor Publisher Services